Narrow butt hole

Erotic BDSM taboo

Erika Sanders

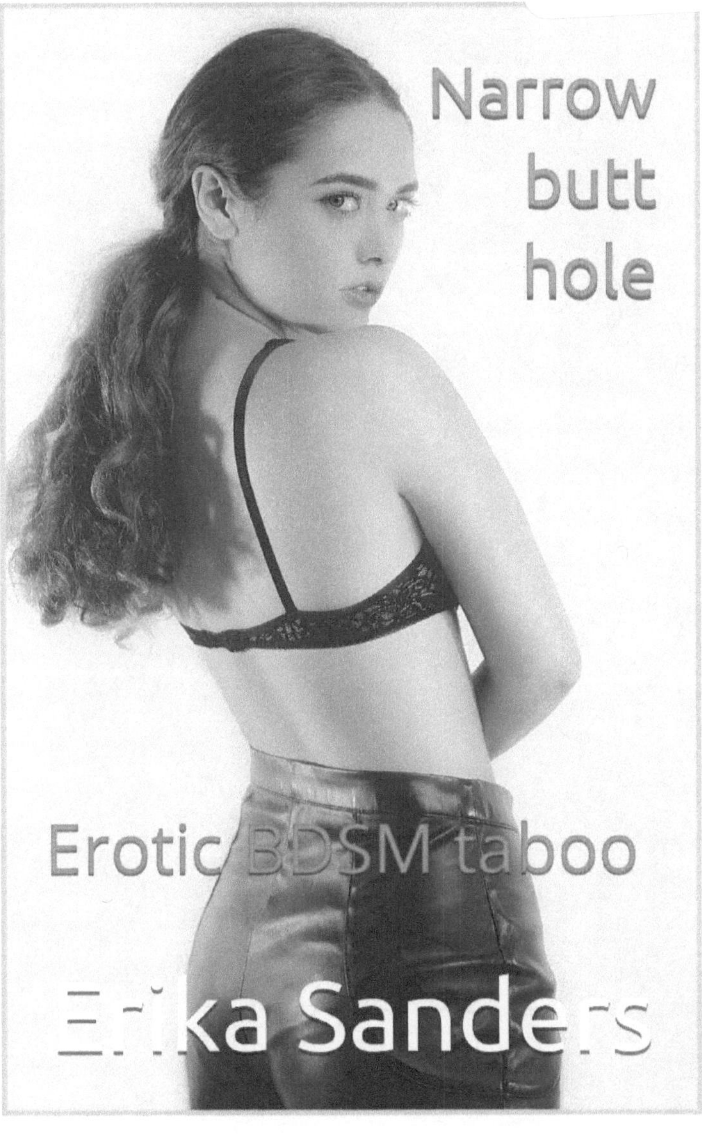

Narrow butt hole
(Erotic BDSM taboo)

Erika Sanders

Serie

Taboo Erotic Collection 3

Synopsis

Enjoy and dominate the tight rear hole ...

The narrow butt hole (erotic taboo) is a story belonging to the Taboo Erotic collection, a series of novels with high erotic content on taboo subjects.

Index:

Synopsis

Note on the author:

Index:

NARROW REAR HOLE (BDSM EROTIC TABO) ERIKA SANDERS

CHAPTER I

CHAPTER II

CHAPTER III

CHAPTER IV

END

NARROW BUTT HOLE
(EROTIC TABOO BDSM)

ERIKA SANDERS

Dick's cock slowly invaded Samantha's wrinkled, lubricated anus and then came out at the same rate. The sensual scene was repeated several times and the warmth of her narrow channel soon made him yearn for more. Trying to ignore his lack of control over the desperately slow speed, he concentrated on his wife as she moved her butt up and down his length. With her wrists and ankles chained to the bed, she had no choice but to embrace the novelty of being used as her sex toy.

The unusual turn of events began the day before. As he was on his way to work, Dick's cell phone rang at exactly 7:10 in the morning, as expected. Even without checking the caller ID, he knew it was his wife, who called every morning at the same time.

Answering the call hands-free, Dick greeted Samantha warmly,

"Hello, baby."

"Hey! Do you miss me already?" Samantha's voice was full of humor, as they had just parted ways an hour earlier.

Dick snorted,

"Of course! Did you read any good stories yet?"

During her morning exercise routine, Samantha enjoyed reading stories on her favorite erotic literature blog. She selected the categories 'Anal' and 'BDSM' and hoped to find the new discoveries every day. If one tickled him, he told Dick, in great detail, during his separate trips to work.

"I actually read a really hot 'Anal' story," she said wistfully. "A husband tied up his wife as punishment, and then he gave her a really hard ride in the ass. It made me super horny."

Catching her not-so-vague hint, Dick's tone was soft,

"Oh really".

"You know ... it's been a while since we've had time to play some kinky games. And ... well ... I've been a very naughty girl lately. I'm pretty sure I deserve punishment," Doing my best to Sounding contrite, she managed to look pained.

Samantha really loved anal sex, which was a blessing for Dick. The problem was, she screamed like a devil during anal orgasms. With the teenage children still at home, their chances of freeing themselves were few and far between.

Knowing that his wife was desperate for kinky sex, Dick took her not-so-subtle invitation in stride. She was right; it had been a long time since they had enjoyed a wild night. In truth, he was surprised that it had taken him so long to propose a secret sex date, and he totally agreed with the direction of their conversation.

Responding to Samantha's obvious wish, Dick did his part. "I will be the judge of whether you really deserve a punishment. Now tell me what you have done," he said in an authoritative tone.

"Well, for one thing, I happen to be speeding right now," Samantha knew it was a weak effort, but this was only the first pitch.

Dick sighed, disappointed, "You are in a hurry every day. That is not really worthy of a punishment."

"Oh", not caring about her mistake, she was ready for the second pitch. "Well, I borrowed $ 30 from your wallet before I went to work."

Dick chuckled, "Ok ... not much of a surprise. Most days I feel like your personal ATM. Is that all?" He asked, expecting more from his resourceful wife.

Having saved the best for last, Samantha was confident that she was on the brink of success,

"So it turns out the Morrisons invited us to dinner on Friday night and I said we'd love to attend."

There was deathly silence for several moments while Dick processed the unwanted news. She knew perfectly well that he didn't enjoy spending time with the Morrisons. Although the wife was a dear friend of Samantha, the husband was socially awkward.

"Little one," said Dick, after clearing his throat out loud, "you really deserve some punishment for this. Let me see what I can do to make room on my schedule tomorrow afternoon."

When Dick used his sex toy nickname, Samantha's pussy tightened. Being at the mercy of her husband, while he used her body for pleasure, was the most exciting.

Fortunately, it would be ready by noon the next day, which was the perfect time.

Dazed by the success, Samantha barely contained her joy,

"Oh boy! Um, I mean ... oh no! Well, I'll have to accept whatever punishment you feel fits the crime. But, my butt has been feeling really bad being left out lately. "

Upset about the upcoming dinner with the Morrisons, Dick decided to taunt his wife as partial revenge.

"Maybe your punishment is to give up anal intercourse," he joked in his more serious voice.

Stunned, Samantha practically choked.

"Baby, punishment must always include anal!"

"You are not in a position to make demands, Little One." Dick maintained his torment, a wry smile on his face. "I'll take your request into consideration, but don't count on getting away with it. This was a pretty serious transgression. I'm getting into work now. We can talk more later."

Discouraged, Samantha replied:

"I love you".

"I love you too," Dick hung up, pleased with himself for giving his wife one.

In her car, Samantha was horrified by the turn of events. Her clever plan to induce a rough anal session had suddenly derailed.

Surely, Dick must know how much he wanted a kinky hard ass session!

Assuming she could convince him to obey, Samantha quickly devised a plan to give him some Margaritas. There was no way he could resist the allure of her eager ass with a heavy hit of tequila to the body and she knew the place that would suit her needs.

CHAPTER II

The next day Samantha and Dick found themselves home just before lunch. When she suggested a quick trip to her favorite Mexican restaurant, he agreed. Not only were the drinks strong, the food was excellent, and most importantly, the service was fast.

As usual, they requested a secluded booth. After sitting down, two of your favorite Margaritas magically appeared on the table and your food order was quickly taken care of. With the preliminaries out of the way, they sipped and relaxed.

Samantha, a very direct person, had no qualms about speaking frankly. Hoping that Dick had forgotten about his absurd idea of withholding anal sex, he decided to try his luck.

"Hey baby, I'm pretty horny. We're going to go crazy tonight," she said, while giving him a suggestive wink.

Dick chuckled, guessing that Samantha was concerned about his threat to avoid anal play. Although he had every intention of drilling her ass long and hard, he thought it would be fun to continue his ruse.

Raising an eyebrow and keeping his poker face up, he said, "Today, we'll keep it low-key. After all, Little One, you deserve punishment."

"Haha, very funny. Get serious and stop fooling around," she said, trying to mask her obvious concern.

Although he was normally a terrible actor, Dick felt confident in his performance. Samantha was genuinely squirming before her very eyes and it was quite entertaining.

Leaning down, he spoke sternly:

"Make no mistake, my decision is made."

"But honey, don't you enjoy fucking my ass while I'm tied to the bed? You can put me on my knees, with my ass lifted and do whatever you want with me." She tried to tempt him by painting an erotic image. "Imagine your hard cock sinking into my little hole ... imagine my screaming when you make me come ... think of my butt squeezing as your cock empties its load into me! Come on, I need you to deliver me a good amount of cum at my back door! Please ...! "

Always impressed by Samantha's anal enthusiasm, Dick's cock immediately stiffened. Oh yeah, I planned to do all of that and more. But for the moment, he was enjoying the charade.

"I've made my decision. Anal, bondage, and punishment are out of the question today," he said, managing to sound disinterested.

Seeing Samantha's face flicker in frustration was immensely amusing for Dick. He expected her to change her strategy and was not disappointed.

Samantha moved quickly, trying to blame him.

"But baby, you're the one who hooked me on anal! If you think about it, this is really your fault. You owe me a good ass fucking!"

There was some truth in his statement. It had taken Dick over twenty years to convince Samantha that anal sex was worth a try. Once she realized that anal orgasms were real and rivaled the vaginal variety, no one stopped her. In a sense, he was responsible for creating this anal monster.

Intrigued to see where he might go next, Dick continued to tug on his chain, "Missionary position and vaginal penetration will do for today, little one."

Samantha's face twisted in disbelief. That kind of sex was fine for weeknights, when they had to be quiet because the kids were home. But this wicked opportunity was too precious to waste!

Determined to try her hand at flattery, Samantha didn't miss a beat.

"Okay, listen. I'm going to be totally honest. If you weren't so good at beating my ass, I wouldn't even want to have anal sex. Skills like yours shouldn't be wasted."

Squinting, Dick's response was simple:

"Nice try".

"Baby please tie me up and fuck my ass! It's been too long since we've played and I really need it," he complained, as a last resort.

Dick shook his head and thought about sympathizing with her. If he confessed to her that it was a joke at her expense, she would calm down. About to speak, she suddenly felt his bare foot directly on her crotch. With her toes, she gently stroked his rock-hard erection under the table as she smiled in victory.

"You keep saying 'no' but your dick says 'hell yeah'. Am I right?" Samantha whispered, her eyes shining with joy.

Suddenly, not wanting to give up, Dick took several deep breaths and tried to focus on unattractive thoughts. Imagining dinner at the Morrisons brought him out of the abyss.

Speaking slowly and softly, he replied:

"My rules today are upheld."

Samantha shrugged and sighed,

"Okay, you win, Baby. Let's enjoy lunch and go home. Hell, maybe we should just relax. You seem a little tense."

Their orders came in and the couple quickly got them to eat, while they discussed other matters. Dick was surprised that Samantha managed to put the conversation behind her, as she didn't like to lose.

In the back of her mind, Samantha felt justified by the preparations made earlier in the day. Dick had chosen to play with fire and he would soon burn. She was fully prepared to act and take his cock up her own ass.

CHAPTER III

When they got home, the couple went straight up to their bedroom. Dick sat on the corner of the bed while Samantha slowly peeled off her jeans and white button-up shirt. Knowing full well that he enjoyed a good striptease, he made sure to exaggerate his movements. As she was about to remove the black lace bra and matching thong, she walked over to her husband and removed her lingerie in front of him.

Standing naked before him, Samantha looked honestly at Dick and asked:

"Honey, can I give you a massage? You deserve one for being so patient with my antics."

Although Dick was ready to beat his wife's butt senseless, Samantha's thoughtful suggestion moved him. Her massages were pretty decent and time-consuming.

"That's a good deal, Little One. Go ahead. But first, undress me."

Blushing sweetly, Samantha replied:

"With pleasure".

Since Dick had left his jacket and tie downstairs, it didn't take long. She climbed onto the bed and crouched directly behind him, putting her knees on either side of his body. Reaching his chest, she unbuttoned his shirt and took it off. His simple white T-shirt followed.

"Get up and turn around," she whispered seductively.

Dick followed her instructions which put his pelvis directly in front of her face. As she looked him in the eye, Samantha unbuckled his belt, unzipped his pants, and then unzipped the zipper. Tugging, she pulled down his pants and underwear, leaving him naked and semi-erect.

"Now, lie back and let my fingers do their work," she said as she tapped the bed.

Happy to comply, Dick stretched out in the middle of the bed, face down. After straddling him, Samantha sat in the center of his back.

Starting at his shoulders, she spoke with concern:

"Oh baby, your arms feel so tight! Put them over your head so I can work all your muscle groups."

Dick was very distracted by the wet spot forming on his back under Samantha's pussy, but he managed to register his request. Stretching his arms toward the pillows, he was vaguely aware that Samantha slid forward, until she was between his shoulder blades. After leaning over the edge of the bed, she seemed to grab something. Then, quick as lightning, he felt cold steel around his wrists and heard the telltale click of the handcuffs.

Dick's head snapped back as he tugged on his hands and found them restricted. Reality hit hard; his slim wife had just dropped him, no small thing since he weighed much more. Immediately afterwards, the agile devil slipped out of his body and sat next to him.

Although reluctant to look at his wife, who was surely proud of the joke, Dick turned his head to the side. What immediately caught his attention was the slippery cunt that was on display between her widely spread thighs. He groaned, feeling foolish for being caught face down.

"Ha! I've totally cheated on you!" she screeched.

Dick knew she would not be content with this, as Samantha was prone to gloating. Being generally calm, he was tempted to join in her rejoicing, but decided to take stock of the situation.

"Nice move, Little One," he conceded, always courteous. "So what happens next?"

Samantha hadn't finished screaming:

"Holy guacamole! I actually captured you! I wish you had seen the expression on your face! Quite a poem!"

"Yeah, you got me seriously. So what's the end of your game?"

Laughing at his involuntary pun, she replied.

"It's more like my 'butt' game!"

Taking several deep breaths, she calmed down. Pleasing Dick was definitely part of the plan and she wanted to reassure him.

"Ok, ok! Ugh! These are your options. I'll attach the handcuffs to a small piece of chain that is secured to the bedpost. That leaves you free to roll onto your back. If you choose that path, I'll get on your cock to put it to good use. But you'll be completely at my mercy for a change. Or ... I can stay here and play with me while you nap. It's totally up to you, love. "

Dick made up his mind immediately, but made a show of reflecting on it,

"Let's see, I can let you use my dick, or lay here like a bundle to snore. I'll go for option number one."

Clapping like a little girl, Samantha was delighted. While she preferred a submissive role during kinky games, Dick pressed a previously unknown hot button by threatening to deny her anal sex. He couldn't blame anyone but himself for her extreme measures.

"Excellent!" She exclaimed. "Now turn around and keep your legs apart. I need to chain your ankles."

Leaning on one elbow, Dick turned his body as Samantha directed. She jumped out of bed and pulled out some metal ankles that she must have hidden under the mattress earlier that day.

Once all of Dick's limbs were restrained, Samantha proudly studied her work. With her gaze fixed on her husband's face, she kissed his forehead tenderly.

"Don't worry, baby. I'll be gentle," she whispered directly into him ear.

Dick, a quiet guy, laughed at the little trickster:

"Well, little one, it seems that you have me right where you wanted me."

"Well, I do have you. Thanks for noticing," she laughed as she headed for the door. "Now, stay still and I'll be right back."

Being restricted was a new experience for Dick. The couple had been involved in slavery from the beginning of their relationship and during their three decades together, Samantha had spent countless hours handcuffed, chained, and even on a stockade. She had never expressed an interest in turning the tables before, so this was an unexpected turn.

Dick was impressed that Samantha took advantage of her great experience to tie him to the bed. Testing him mobility, he was truly proud that she had managed to secure him without causing him pain.

The handcuffs were not too tight on him wrists / ankles, nor were him limbs stretched to the point of discomfort. All in all, it was quite a successful endeavor.

His attention shifted after noticing that Samantha had returned and was standing in the middle of the room.

To say that she had dressed for the occasion would have been an understatement.

CHAPTER IV

"You like what you see?" Samantha's eyes sparkled mischievously as she modeled for him in her new outfit.

Usually she preferred soft, feminine lingerie, but this afternoon she had gone in a new direction. A strapless black leather corset gave her the look of a woman in control. Already small, it accentuated her tiny waist even more, while managing to make her small breasts appear larger. She opted to go pantiesless, leaving her hairless sex exposed for her viewing pleasure. A little lower, to the thigh, sheer black stockings hugged her toned legs. Completing the erotic ensemble she wore stern-looking black stilettos.

Dick's jaw hung open staring in amazement at the appearance of his wife, dressed in such a daring outfit.

"Shit! You look SO hot, Little One!"

Pulling away from him, she tilted her hips to the side and patted her bottom. With his cock now shaped into a full mast, he briefly struggled to get up before he remembered that he was tied to the bed.

"Little one, let me get up and I'll give your ass the hardest ride of your life," he said, trying to negotiate.

Samantha shook her head as she laughed,

"Oh I'm going to have a rough ride, don't worry. You had your chance and you blew it. I'm planning to take what I want on my own."

"Come on! I was just joking about withholding anal sex. Let's change places," he begged.

Samantha shrugged and replied:

"You hit the wrong key, baby. What's done is done. Now if you insist on talking, there will be consequences."

"But," he began.

"Exactly! But ..." she replied, making quotation marks with her fingers. "That's the name of this game. Now, I warned you to shut up and disobey."

Samantha touched the side of her mouth with her index finger and narrowed her eyes in false concentration.

"Let's see, how should I deal with your disobedience? Hey, I have an idea," he said, waving his hands seriously. "Instead of spluttering, you should use your mouth to please me!"

Feeling that the game was well under way, Dick was not sure if he should respond verbally. Wisely, he chose to nod his head in agreement. Samantha's outrageous outfit and obscene demeanor made him crave any kind of contact with her body.

"Ah, I see you are a fast learner," she said. "Let's put your mouth to work. I want you to lick my naughty hole, like a good boy."

Once again, Dick nodded emphatically, happy to agree. Allowing Samantha this 'role reversal' moment seemed just right under the circumstances and he was happy to accompany her on the journey.

Carefully not to push her husband, Samantha crawled back onto the bed. She straddled him at his neck and knelt down, placing her rear directly over his face. Always teasing, she turned her pelvis as she rubbed her hands along the smooth curves of her buttocks.

"Now give me some pleasure ... in my butt," she said with authority.

Samantha felt Dick's body shake from the laughter he fought to suppress. Kissing his wife wasn't really a punishment and watching her get horny while he licked her ass was arousing. Consequently, he was more than happy to please her.

Smiling, Samantha leaned down and looked between her legs,

"I'm giving you access to a very special place, Baby."

As if revealing a precious gift, she moved her hands to the center of her toned butt and parted her creamy white buttocks. There, for Dick's viewing pleasure, was her delicate star. In the light of day, he could easily appreciate each and every one of the folds that made up her nameless entrance. Slightly darker than the rest of her skin, the tone gave her an almost exotic look. Overall, it was a very attractive target and he never tired of hitting it.

Misinterpreting his pause, Samantha spoke words of encouragement:

"Come on, baby. You know what to do. Put your mouth on my ass."

With pleasure, Dick pursed his lips and pressed them against Samantha's anus, which was now trembling with anticipation. Affectionately, he nibbled, sucked, and kissed her way around the small circle, eliciting soft moans from his wife. He wasn't an amateur, he knew exactly how to handle the wrinkled skin around her back door.

Samantha was eternally in awe of the pleasure she experienced during anal stimulation. In her mind, it proved that anal sex was a natural sexual act, that it did not deserve its taboo status. Before long, the exquisite feel of his mouth melting against her opening had her poised and yearning for more.

"Baby ... please! Slide your tongue up my ass and make me cum." she moaned.

She didn't need to say it twice. Dick was an extremely generous lover and he hoped to push her to the limit. Sticking out his tongue, he stiffened it as much as he could, before appropriately invading the hole brazenly offered by his wife.

To help, Samantha slowly lowered her body until her tongue barely peeked through the taut entrance to her place of pleasure. The searing heat within her sensitive edge affected her so deeply that it momentarily stole her breath. Craving a full penetration, Samantha began her final descent onto his mouth.

"Fuck baby. That feels so good! Oooooh!" Samantha began to move her ass on him relentless tongue.

Dick picked up on her obvious cues and went for taste. Slowly but surely, his tongue achieved maximum intimate contact. As usual, her external sphincter accepted his intrusion after some initial resistance. Once past that barrier, he pushed forward, deep enough to cross her most inflexible internal sphincter.

"Aaahhhh! Baby! Please! Make me cum!"

Although significantly smaller than his cock, Dick's tongue made up for the size discrepancy with his dexterity. He alternated between rolling his tongue and shoving in and out of her most private place. In no rush, he was happy to assuage her need. Judging from the amount of pussy juice that was pooling on his chin, he knew she would soon climax.

As Dick worked his magic on her butt, Samantha was beside herself. She had waited, with some impatience, for this moment all day. Feeling his sensual lips and talented tongue on her intimate area sent a wave of relief through her body. At the same time, the sexual tension that had been building was on the verge of exploding. It was an interesting contrast that she enjoyed.

After spending several minutes tending to Samantha's carnal urges, Dick felt her posture change. Arching her back, she began to slowly move up and down over his face, while still holding her buttocks open for his tongue. She was close to arriving and he braced himself for what was to come next.

Suddenly, she stiffened. In a desperate attempt to find support, she moved her hands to his chest, leaving his face between her thankfully small buttocks. Barely able to breathe, he bravely pushed on.

Time seemed to stop as Samantha hurtled off the orgasmic cliff. What started as a small spark located in the center of her anus soon spread like wild fire throughout her body. In that split second, every muscle in her pelvis began to contract and relax rhythmically as the blessed release claimed her.

"Ooohhh God!" She howled at the top of her lungs, her head thrown back in ecstasy.

After several seconds, Samantha went limp and fell forward onto Dick's abdomen, pulling his butt out of his face. Muttering, she seemed momentarily incoherent, but managed to move and stay by his side with her head resting on his chest. Stroking him, she purred like a satisfied sex kitten.

Susan, already more relaxed, finally murmured:

"Baby, that felt amazing. You can talk now, if you want.

"Nope. I'm fine," was his arrogant reply.

Looking at his face, she snickered,

"Really? Is there nothing you want to say?"

His only response was to shake his head with a puzzled expression. Sometimes the words just weren't necessary.

Accepting Dick's vow of silence, Samantha's focus abruptly shifted when she noticed his cock swinging proudly between her thighs. Elegantly covered with a drop of precum, it called her on a sexual level. Although exhausted from the force of her recent climax, she needed his cock in her ass and she would settle for nothing less. Spurred on by her undeniable desire, she reached out and grasped his throbbing manhood with both hands.

"Hmmm, you'll be talking very soon," she answered confidently as she stroked his cock and filled it with saliva.

In general, Samantha was not a fan of being on top and preferred to absorb the force of Dick's male power during intercourse. Realizing that this was her dominant moment to shine, she decided on the position that would give Dick the best view. After taking off her shoes, she slid forward and squatted, staring at his feet. Balancing on her knees, her ass hovered tantalizingly over his erection.

Samantha needed real anal satisfaction, and now the time had come.

"Get ready, Baby. I'm going to rape your cock with my ass," she whispered in a voice tinged with lust.

Reaching behind her, she grabbed his cock with her right hand and used the other to pull her left buttock to the side. With precision, she aligned his manhood against her hungry hole and rubbed his head at her entrance. The combination of his precum and her saliva was an effective lubricant and she knew from experience that it would be enough to ease her passage.

Dick felt his clamp when his cock poked out. Carefully, she proceeded to mount it until she was fully seated at her rear entrance. Although far from his first anal experience, Dick still appreciated the extraordinary view of Samantha's ass, as it wrapped his cock. Never tiring of the powerful image, he only wished she could achieve his point of view.

Clinging tightly to her warm flesh, he yearned for the sweet friction that came from advancing wildly in and out of the narrow canal. But for now, he was content to let Samantha drive and bide his time.

After moaning throughout the insertion and adjustment period, Samantha finally spoke with great pride:

"Baby look! I shoved you deep in my ass, by myself!"

The presence of Dick's thick member on her butt always put Samantha in orbit, as the stretch of her sensitive tissue was almost enough to induce an orgasm. However, being on the edge of Nirvana was not as good as getting there. There was still work to be done. Placing both hands on his thighs and arching her back, she prepared herself for the final round.

She began to rise and fall on his hard length with determination. At first, it was intentional, while trying to adjust at a reasonable pace. Trying to pick up speed, she found that it was quite a challenge without Dick's help. Gracefully, she managed to switch to her sensation without dislodging his cock. But it soon became clear that her small stature made it impossible to achieve the punishment rate she so desired.

After several minutes of Samantha's efforts, Dick's desperation became unbearable. Although he enjoyed this appetizer, his cock was ravenous for the main course. Still, he held back and waited for her to pass the witness to him.

"Baby, I ... this ... is ... difficult," she finally admitted, unable to get on with her own ass.

Dick was more than ready to retake the position of dominant state. During Samantha's next lowering, he unexpectedly moved his hips. Consequently, Samantha fell backwards, while still impaled on his cock. Landing with her back against his chest, she tried and couldn't straighten up. Dick waited while she moved for a few seconds, making sure she was stable in position.

"Now tell me, Little One, who's in charge," he whispered.

Relieved by the help, Samantha's request was simple:

"For the love of God, just carve me out, baby."

Dick finally let go of her needy ass when he was satisfied with her position. Jumping like a bronco, he struck her fiercely from below as she held her pelvis slightly above his. Her screams, moans, and pleas for "MORE" were like music to his ears. His wife really loved anal sex … of that he was sure.

Now that Dick was giving her what she so badly needed, Samantha was in heaven. Despite their relative positions, she gladly allowed him to claim her body, making it his own. Big and powerful, his cock affected her in a way that his tongue couldn't and the depths to which he sank her inner walls soon prepared her for another climax. Hearing him growl as he found pleasure in her butt finally pushed Samantha to the limit.

"Please! Not Stop!" She begged.

Having sensed his wife on the precipice, Dick was soon rewarded for his frantic efforts. When he finally succumbed, her ass squeezed his cock with superhuman strength. Once her rhythmic contractions began, he allowed a well-deserved orgasm to take over his body. Stream after stream of his seed gushed into her hard lust as he screamed her name with lustful pleasure.

Already at the peak of her body spasms, Samantha had an emotional climax when he called her by name. There was no greater reward than inducing Dick to orgasm with one of hers and she thrived on this sexual rush. Instinctively, she gripped his hips like an anchor as their bodies trembled in unison.

Samantha collapsed on top of him after weathering the sexual tsunami. She groped for several seconds before trying to disconnect from the source of her sexual satisfaction. The consummate

'Dirty Girl' enjoyed his cum on her ass and wanted to save what she could. Surprisingly, she managed to get up and twist everything in one motion, spreading out the length of her body. Sated, Dick was content to let himself relax, though he was still restrained by the handcuffs.

As she listened to his slow heart rate, Samantha sensed that he might be asleep and decided that she could set her afternoon sex toy free.

Briefly, she wondered if he would seek revenge. With all her heart, she expected it ...

Only time would tell.

END